The Trouble with Gran

Babette Cole

Mammoth

The trouble with Gran is . . .

. . . secretly . . .

she's
an
alien!

None of the other OAPs suspected a thing . . .

. . . until our teacher tried to organise an outing for them, to Wethorp, as our school project!

"Sit down and be quiet!" snapped teacher.

Wethorp was awful.

Gran started to play up!

We went to an Old Time Music Hall.

Gran did not like the singing!

And there was a Glamorous Grandma Contest .

. . . Gran cheated of course!

She really
livened up
the fun fair!

We were asked to leave the amusement arcade!

On the Lunar Landscape Tour
Gran met some friends.

She took them to the tea rooms!

So we missed the bus home.

Teacher blamed Gran!

"We've had enough of this dump!" said Gran.
"Fasten safety-belts!"

We zoomed towards Gran's planet . . .

and landed just in time
for carnival!

PLANET GRAN
CARNIVAL
1988

Gran did the Limbo . . .

. . . and climbed a bloomernut tree.

We were sad to leave,
but Gran had to get home
to feed the cat.

We landed in the school playground with a bump!

Mum and Dad marched Gran away.
"You're too old for that sort of thing now,"
they said.

"That's what they think," muttered Gran.

And when she got home she opened her own travel agency . . .

. . . in Dad's garage!

First published in Great Britain 1987
by William Heinemann Ltd
This edition published 1997
by Mammoth
an imprint of Reed Consumer Books Ltd.
Michelin House, 81 Fulham Road, London SW3 6RB
and Auckland, Melbourne, Singapore and Toronto

10 9 8 7 6 5 4 3 2 1

ISBN 0 7497 1026 8

A CIP catalogue record for this title
is available from the British Library

Produced by Mandarin Offset Ltd
Printed and bound in Hong Kong